Snakebite

by

Robert Swindells

First published in 2006 in Great Britain by
Barrington Stoke Ltd
18 Walker St, Edinburgh EH3 7LP

www.barringtonstoke.co.uk

Reprinted 2007

ISBN: 978-1-84299-415-3

Printed in Great Britain by Bell & Bain Ltd

A Note from the Author

I once worked with a man who had an extreme fear of snakes. We worked on a local newspaper in the middle of Bradford, so there wasn't much chance that we would ever really meet a snake. But poor Fred (that was my friend's name) only had to see a picture of a snake, or hear someone talking about them, and he'd go dead white. He'd start to sweat and have to sit down. Then he'd shiver and have to take little sips of water. He'd feel terrible.

Everyone thought Fred must have once had a bad experience with a snake. In fact he'd never been near one. His extreme fear of snakes puzzled him as much as it puzzled us. He never got over it. Snakes terrified him all his life.

I was thinking about Fred when I got the idea for *Snakebite*. But I haven't dedicated the book to him. He'd have hated that.

So – cheers, Fred. No snakes where you are now, I bet.

For Sam, Greg and Amelia

Contents

Chapter 1
One Bad Thing

Is there one bad thing in your life? Something that makes you think, *If only that one thing was out of my life, I'd be really, really happy*?

There's something bad in most people's lives. There is in mine. My bad thing is called Mark Burn.

Mark's the guy who calls me Cow. I'm Alex Cowan but he called me Cow, because cows can't read and I'm not all that good at it myself. This was when we were at school. I've left now and so has Mark. I thought he'd leave me alone once we left school, but I couldn't have been more wrong.

Mark's got a gang now. The Ointment. That's what they call themselves, don't ask me why. Ointment's what you put on cuts and bangs to make them better, but Mark's Ointment *gives* you cuts and bruises. I try to stay out of Mark's way, but our flats are on the same estate and I keep bumping into him and his gang.

Mark Burn has no work to go to. Neither do his pals. They hang out and look for people to hassle. Anybody will do – kids, lasses, old ladies. The Ointment will have a go at anyone who can't hit back. They act hard but they're not stupid. No way will the Ointment hassle anyone who might hurt *them*.

I'm no hard man – wish I was. "Hello, Cow!" Mark'll shout as I creep by. "Come over here and be milked." Don't ask. What he means is that he's going to grab me where it hurts and squeeze. It hurts so much, I can't keep from crying. To avoid milking I'll start to run. If I'm lucky the Ointment'll just shout and jeer at me as I get away. If they're feeling fit and fast, they'll come after me, and if I don't get to a street where there are other people around, witnesses, it's milking time.

So that's my one bad thing. I have to sneak about the place and try to dodge the Ointment while I look for work. It feels as if my life'll be like this forever and ever but it won't. It won't, because something amazing is about to happen. Stick around if you want to know what.

Chapter 2
Guppies

I breed guppies. Guppies are small fish. They're tropical fish so you need a heated tank to keep them in. They come in all different colours, but the best thing about them is, they have babies. Most fish lay eggs, but guppies are born alive and swimming. You've got to have plenty of plants in your tank for the babies to hide in, or the adult guppies will eat them.

Guppy's another name that Mark Burn calls me. I don't know who told him, but he found out I breed guppies and he thinks it's really funny. "Hello, Guppy!" he'll shout. "Have your guppies had puppies?" His mates fall about when he says this, like he's the wittiest guy on the planet. It's another excuse to rough me up while the Ointment snap pictures with their phones.

I like animals. Always have. They're better than people if you ask me. I was always the one who fed the school gerbils and cleaned out their cage. No prize for guessing what Burn called me. Gerbil, of course. "Come on, Gerbil," he used to say, as he pushed me over in the playground, "Let's hear you burble like a gerbil." That would make his girlfriend laugh really loud. "You're such a laugh, Burnie," she'd hoot as I rolled in the dust around Mark Burn's feet. That was bad, because Burn's girlfriend was Kirsty Simpson and she's drop-dead gorgeous. I fancied the hell out of her. Still do.

And I still can't see what's wrong with liking animals.

The night before my seventeenth birthday, my Uncle Dan comes to our flat with a cardboard box. "Happy birthday, Alex," he goes. "Sorry it's not gift-wrapped." He puts the box on the floor and watches me open it. Ma and Dad are watching too. I pull up the flaps and jump back. There's a snake in it.

Ma's like, "Ugh!" but Uncle Dan laughs. "It won't hurt you," he says. "It's a garter snake from America. They're not poisonous, and they make interesting pets."

"Fantastic," I gasp, now I'm over the shock. "It's a wicked present, Uncle Dan. Thanks. I mean it."

"I know you do, Alex," he smiles. "And I know she's come to a good home."

I look at him. "She?"

He nods. "Yes, it's a female. You'll need to give her a name."

I keep on looking into the box, can't take my eyes off my latest pet. She's mostly red, with black markings. She's all coiled up now but if she wasn't, she'd be about 50cm long. "Flicka," I breathe.

"What?" goes Uncle Dan.

I grin. "I'm calling her Flicka."

"Why Flicka?" says Dad.

"'Cos of the way her tongue flicks in and out all the time," I tell him.

"What do they eat?" asks Ma.

"Mothers," says Uncle Dan. He's a million times more witty than Mark Burn. Ma squeals.

"No." Uncle Dan laughs and shakes his head. "That's a joke. They like rats, frogs and crickets. Alive."

Dad pulls a face. "Where's Alex going to find live crickets round Bellfield, Dan?" Bellfield's the name of the estate we live on.

"They sell 'em down the shop," says Uncle Dan. "Rab's Reptiles. That's where I bought her."

When my uncle's gone, I fetch a spare fishtank from the lobby cupboard. I got the spare tank before I knew the baby guppies just needed plants to hide in when the big guppies were trying to eat them. I would always put the babies in their own tank before I worked that one out. Then I get a heating lamp and a lump of rock. With those in it, the tank makes a pretty good home for a snake. I carry the tank to my room, set it down on the desk next to the iMac and plug in the heating lamp. Flicka curls round the rock and seems to settle in fine.

Next morning I make sure she's survived the night, then set off to Rab's Reptiles for snake food. Ma's like, "Ask for the crickets, son. I don't want live rats in my flat. Or frogs."

My head's so full of Flicka, I don't even think about Mark Burn. I stride along like there's no such thing as the Ointment. Shame it can't be like this every day.

It's my first time in Rab's Reptiles. Cool shop. There are loads of tanks all along the walls. In the tanks are lizards, snakes and big furry spiders. It's wild.

"What can I get you, son?" growls the guy at the far end. He's a big fella. I don't think he's happy I'm using his shop like a zoo. He doesn't like people looking and not buying. I can imagine him saying, "Pick a window, pal, you're leaving."

"My uncle bought a garter snake from you yesterday," I tell him.

He scowls at me. *"And?"*

"It was for me – for my birthday."

"So?"

"So I need some food," I say.

He glares. "For you, or the snake?"

"The ... the snake, of course." Is he trying to be funny?

"Rats, mice, frogs, crickets," he snarls. I don't think he's being funny.

"My ma wants the crickets," I tell him.

He nods. "And what about the snake?"

"Ah – she'd like the crickets too, I'm sure."

He gets my crickets. They come in a plastic box with a lid. “Four quid,” he mutters. “Keep the lid on if you don’t want a houseful of the wee beasties.”

I peer at the box. “How long will they live?”

“Till the snake gets ’em.” There’s not even the ghost of a smile as he says it. I cram the box in my hoody and go.

I’m so busy thinking about Rab and his reptile shop, I don’t see the Ointment. I really do bump into them. “My, aren’t we bright and early?” says Burn. “What’s that in your pocket, Cow?”

Chapter 3
Cost Me Four Quid

"It's nothing," I tell him. "Just a box."

He smirks. "Empty, is it?"

I nod. "Yes."

"Yeah, right." He turns to his pals. "Do we believe him, lads?"

Zac Doyle shakes his head. "*I* don't, Burnie."

"Me neither," goes Andy Crockett. "He's mooing 'cos it's milking time."

Jimmy Farr just looks at me.

Mark nods. "I think you're right, Andy. Grab 'im."

In a flash Doyle's behind me, his arm round my neck. I cry out as Crockett grabs and squeezes. Mark stands with his hands in his pockets and smiles. "Get the box, Jimmy," he orders. Jimmy Farr dodges my kicks, shoves his hand in my hoody pocket and pulls out the box. The pain's so bad, I'm yelling, half-blind with tears. There's nothing I can do to stop it. At least Kirsty's not here to see.

"Hey, see this, lads?" Mark's got the plastic box and he's holding it up to the light. "It's full of wee beasties, so it is." He's about to pull off the lid.

"Don't!" I choke. "They'll escape." Crockett lets go of me a moment because he's watching Mark. Mark looks at me. "What are they, Cow?" The lid's half off.

"Crickets," I gasp. "They cost me four quid. Don't let 'em ..."

It's no good, of course. "Crickets?" Mark says. Then he turns the box upside down and shakes it. The insects whirr away on the breeze. "Nasty wee creatures," he cries. "Guppies're bad enough without you breeding crickets all over the estate as well."

I don't know what the Ointment were going to do next. Just then a police car noses round the corner. Doyle and Crockett let go at once and I fall to the ground. By the time the car's right round the corner, I'm the only one there.

"You all right, son?" goes the policeman. He gives me a hand and I stand up and dust myself down.

I nod my head. “Aye.”

He looks at me. “D’you know those guys?”

“Never seen ’em before.” He knows I’m lying, but he understands why. Lads like Burn tend to deal a bit of crack to make their dole money go a bit further. When you do that, there’s scary pals in the background – guys who’ll do someone in as soon as spit. The policeman gets back in the car, which zooms away.

I pick the box out of the gutter and waste a few minutes looking for my crickets. No chance, of course. They were snake feed, now they’re free. If I was one of them, you wouldn’t see me for dust.

I’m sore in a couple of places, but that’s not the worst thing. The worst thing is, I’ve got to go and see Rab again. Mr Happy.

“You were gone a while,” goes Ma when I walk in at last.

"Aye." I drop the box on the table. "He had to send to China to get these." No point telling my mother about the Ointment, she'd only fret.

He's a crook, that Rab. He didn't give me a discount even though I had my own box *and* he talked me into forking out for a bag of sand as well. "Snakes don't lie on glass," he says. "Not in the wild. They're happiest lying on sand. Hot sand. If you want to keep a snake, it's down to you to see she's happy." He slides the bag of sand across the counter. "Two-twenty-five."

I goggle. "£2.25 for *sand*?"

"Special stuff. I imported it just for the snakes." He shrugs. "A comfy snake is a happy snake."

Crook, I think. I lift Flicka out of the tank, slip her into my pocket. I take out the rock, pour in the sand, level it off. I work quickly. Flicka might not be too happy in my pocket.

Then I put back the rock, bed it in the sand. Flicka's not wriggling around or anything. In fact, when I pull her out she seems really relaxed. I put her back in the tank, on her special sand. She doesn't look any happier than before, but it's not easy to tell with a snake. I drop a cricket in and put the lid back on the tank. The lid'll stop the cricket getting away and you've got to have it anyway. It's where the heating lamp is.

It's my birthday, so I'm off out tonight with the oldies. There's this comedy club that has shows. You know – stand-up comics and that. It's an oldies' club. I wish I was off to a *real* club with Kirsty Simpson, but I can't dance and anyway I don't have the right kit.

It's a while before we need to set off, so I put some music on and lie on my bed and watch Flicka.

Chapter 4
You're Dead

I've done really well for birthday money. Sixty quid. The next day's Saturday. I decide to check out the clothes shops down town. I fancy one of those coats they've brought out that have big, stick-up collars. If you wear a dressy scarf with a coat like that, you look pretty cool. Like one of those 70s glam-rock guys. Sixty quid's not enough, of course, but I've got a bit saved up as well. You never know – Kirsty Simpson might look at me twice in cool kit.

There's no sign of the cricket in Flicka's tank, so she's eating all right. That's a relief. It means she's settled in. I touch the glass near her face and say, "*See ya*," then I remember how laid-back she was in my pocket yesterday. "Hey, Flicka," I murmur. "What d'you say you and me take a little walk down town, eh?" I *know* I'm acting the numpty, but what the heck.

It's a dry morning. I leave my hoody unzipped. The snake's weight makes the pocket swing to and fro as I walk. I bet Flicka's enjoying the movement, like rocking in a hammock. And I'm enjoying her company. Everything's fine till I look over a rail of coats in Next and see Mark Burn walk in.

What the heck's *he* doing in Next, today of all days? I can't believe my rotten luck. I duck down, as if I'm looking at something at the bottom of the coats. I watch him through a gap. He hasn't spotted me but he's coming this way. I move to the end of the rail. I've ducked right down. I'll slip away as soon as Mark stops to look at something in the shop.

He does stop, but just then a load of shouting breaks out near the entrance. It's Jimmy Farr. He drags a shirt out of a carrier bag and starts shouting. "Cheaters!" he yells. "Yous're nothing but a bunch of low, lying cheaters. See this?" He waves the shirt over his head. "*Machine wash*, it says on the tab, and it comes out lookin' like ..."

I'm so busy gawping across at Jimmy, I forget I'm meant to be hiding from Mark. I remember, and turn my head in time to see him putting on his old jacket over one he's just nicked off a rail.

I don't shout or point or anything. I mind my own business when Mark Burn's around. But before I can duck down again, one of the lasses who works in the shop calls out, dashes across and grabs Mark's sleeve. As she does this, he turns and sees me looking. He looks right back at me and mouths, "*You're dead, Cowan.*"

I open my hands, shrug and shake my head. *I didn't do anything*, I mouth back.

Jimmy's vanished. I want to vanish too but there's no chance. The shop's security arrive. Two big fellas come up and take hold of Burn. The lass points to me. "He saw him take it."

"No, I didn't." I shake my head.

"Why would she say you did if you didn't?" one of the security guys growls.

"*I* don't know," I tell him.

"Maybe you was *in* on it, too, eh, like the fella with the shirt?"

"No." I shake my head again. "I just happened to turn round when he was putting his jacket back on."

"Ah," goes the big guy. "So you *did* see?"

Sometimes you can't win. I nod. The guy asks for my name and address. I'll be called as a witness, he tells me. *Aye, right*, I think to myself, *if I'm still breathing*.

I don't buy a coat and scarf. I'm not in the mood. I leave the shop. As I walk home I have my hand in my pocket and I stroke

Flicka. People think snakes're cold and slimy but they're not. They're dry and warm. I love the feel of her in my pocket, and she seems not to mind being there. How many other guys in the world take their snakes for a walk?

Sunday morning I go down the paper shop to return a DVD and pick one for tonight. I don't take Flicka. It's cold, and last night's cricket is still in the tank. I'm even more nervous than most days, because I know what Mark Burn said to me yesterday. He definitely said *you're dead.* Lucky for me, he doesn't seem to be around. I'm nearly home when Jimmy Farr steps out of a doorway and makes me jump.

"Message from Burnie," he says. "Enjoy your legs while you can."

"W-what does *that* mean?" I stammer.

Jimmy smiles. "Means he's gonna smash 'em sometime soon, Cow. Oh, and here's something from me. The police don't know who the fella with the shirt was, and it better stay like that. If not, you'll get your elbows smashed as well."

I picked a gangster movie for tonight, but I seem to have gone off it a bit. Know what I mean?

Chapter 5
No Place To Hide

"Something bothering you, son?" goes my mother. It's Sunday night. I can't settle.

"No, Ma," I lie.

"Only you're up and down like a jack-in-the-box," she says. "Your dad and me can't concentrate on the film."

"I'm fine, Ma. I'm not in the mood for gangsters, that's all."

I know I'm a pain. I've been in and out of the room about six times since my mother put the DVD on. I can't help it. There's another DVD inside my head, one that stars Mark Burn and the Ointment. It keeps playing the same clip. I'm in a dark place, walking. I know something bad's about to happen, but I can't do anything to stop it. I approach a shadowy doorway. The camera cuts to the doorway. Burn and his pals are there. It's an ambush, and I'm walking right into it.

"You chose the film, son," says Dad. "If you're not interested, go play with that snake of yours. You're doing your mother's head in."

"Yeah, OK." I get up and go to my room. The film in my head comes with me. I don't turn out the light in my room. Instead, I slump in my swivel chair and gaze into the tank.

I have to admit the tank's better with the sand. Looks like the desert. The lamp's the sun. The rock sits in a pool of its own shadow. Flicka lies coiled round the rock. Her body's in shade, her head's in the light. Does she think she really is *in* the desert, or does she know she's a prisoner in a tank? Either way, she seems not to care. Too small a brain, maybe.

Mark Burn'll care about being a prisoner. *His* brain's not all that big either, but he'll know he's a prisoner all right. And he'll know I put him there 'cos he'll see me in court. I've got to be a witness.

I groan. Can't get it out of my head, even when I'm watching Flicka. And I'm scared.

Parents. You're supposed to go to your parents if something's worrying you, right? It's what they're *for*. But they grew up in a different world, your parents. Talk to them about a guy like Mark Burn, they'll think you're talking about a bit of pushing and shoving, bit of name-calling, maybe the odd smack. They won't think *baseball bat, knife, gun.* Oh, they've read about that stuff in the papers, but it's not stuff that happens *here*, to folks like *us*.

The cricket's gone, I've just noticed. Don't know when, no idea how. Must be horrible, trapped in a tank with a hungry snake after you. It's the first time I've thought of it from the cricket's point of view. There you sit under the lamp. There's no way out. You're helpless, no place to hide. Doomed no matter what. How must that feel?

Hey, who am I kidding? I know *exactly* how it feels. I'm just like that cricket. Trapped.

Monday mornings I have to go to the Job Centre, sign on. They should just call it the Centre. There are never any jobs, but if you don't show up they stop your benefit. I never like going, because I've always got to dodge the Ointment. Now, with Mark Burn after my legs, it's a hundred times worse.

"They'll maybe have a job for you today, son," goes Ma as I zip up my hoody.

"Aye, Ma," I says. "Bed-tester, no experience necessary, school leavers welcome, fifty grand a year." I've got Flicka in my pocket, but Ma doesn't know. She'd say I was daft.

I make it to the bus stop. I'm all right now, there are other people waiting. Still, I'm glad when the bus comes. I sit looking out of the window, and stroke Flicka in secret. She's getting a free ride.

Ma must be psychic. Lass at the Centre says, "A new job's just come in, Mr Cowan. Sounds just your sort of thing."

I look at her. "Oh aye?"

"Yes." She smiles. "It's part-time, but it's near to where you live."

"What sort of work?" I ask.

"Retail," she says.

I pull a face. "D'you mean shop work? What would I be selling?"

She grins. "Reptiles."

"Don't tell me." I put both my hands up to my head. "It's Rab's Reptiles, right? On Cameron Street."

"That's right." She gives a big smile. "Couldn't be handier, could it? The interview's at eleven. Just show the owner of the shop this card."

"Er, hold on a sec." I shake my head. "I'm not going there. Wouldn't work for that guy if he was the last boss on the planet."

She frowns. "Why not, may I ask?"

"Why *not?*" I cry. "'Cause he's one of the most miserable old so-and-sos I've ever met, that's why. *And* he's a crook."

The girl's smile vanishes. "You can't go saying things like that about people, Mr Cowan. And if you won't go to an interview that's been offered, it could affect your benefit."

My laugh sounds like a bark. "You mean you'll stop my dosh?"

"Well, yes." She nods. "This is a *Job* Centre, Mr Cowan. It isn't a *Sign Your Name and Get Beer Money for Life* Centre. Here." She slides the card with the job details on it across to me. "Eleven o'clock."

Me? Work for that Rab? In your dreams, Miss Stuck Up Smarmy Face. I don't say this to her, of course. I mutter it to myself as I walk out of the Centre with the job card in my hand. I go to stuff the thing in my pocket and Flicka's there. I'd forgotten about her.

"We'll not work for that crook, will we, girl?" I whisper. Flicka doesn't reply and I take that as a no. "We'll go to his rotten interview, but he's not going to want us, is he?"

Chapter 6
Happy To Serve

Rab watches me come up to the counter. "The crickets escaped again, then, did they?" He remembers me as the guy who bought two lots of crickets in an hour. It must have made his twisted little day.

I shake my head. "I've come about the job."

"Ah." He rubs his hands together. "Fancy working with reptiles, eh?"

Another shake of my head. "Not much."

He scowls. "Why're you here, then?"

I shrug. "Job Centre told me I had to come for an interview. Said they'd stop my dosh if I didn't."

"Huh!" Rab looks me up and down. "Not the best reason to apply for a job, is it? Worked in a shop before, have you? Any retail experience?"

"I go in shops."

He frowns. "*This* side of the counter, I mean. Ever serve the public? Er – *what's* your name?" he asks.

"Alex. Alex Cowan," I answer. "And no, I've never served the public. Maybe I could pick that up from you ... ?"

Rab doesn't think so. "Not as easy as it looks, you know. You need to know your stock, for a start. You have to know where everything is. You couldn't let things escape, like you did with those crickets. Got to be polite, too. Helpful. Need to look cheerful, happy to serve."

"Like yourself, you mean?"

"Aye." He peers at me. "D'you find this funny, Alex? Only you seem to be smirking."

"I'm being cheerful, Mr ... er?" I stop, don't know his second name.

"Baxter," he says. "Rab Baxter, but it'd be *Mr* Baxter to you, of course, if you got the job."

"Aye, right." I nod. "I never smirk, Mr Baxter. I'm being cheerful, that's all. Happy to serve."

"Fine." He looks round the shop. "Is there anything you'd like to ask me, Alex?"

"Aye. Would there be a problem with me getting some time off?"

"*What?*" Rab frowns. "You want time off before you've even got the job?"

I nod. "Aye, well, you see, I've got to appear in court, and I don't know exactly when."

"Court?" He narrows his eyes. "What're you going to court for?"

"Oh – it's a shoplifting thing."

"*Shoplifting*?" Old Rab looks like he might explode. "You're due in court for shoplifting, and you expect me to offer you a job in my shop? Get out of here before I call the police."

"OK, Mr Baxter, only I'll be back for crickets sometimes."

"Aye." He nods. "And I'll keep my eye on you, son. Every minute."

I grin. "A cheerful eye, I hope. Happy to serve."

I go back to the Centre. I have to wait. The lass is talking to some guy. As soon as she's free, I go over. She looks up, says, "How'd it go?"

I pull a face. "He didn't want to know, that Rab. Just 'cos I said about going to court."

She frowns. "Court?"

I nod. "Aye."

"What court?" she snaps. "You didn't say anything about court to me."

I shake my head. "I didn't think I'd need to. I'll only be a witness, you see."

"Did you tell Mr Baxter that?"

"No, he didn't give me chance. He just about chucked me out the shop."

"Ah." She nods. "Well, better luck next time, eh, Mr Cowan?"

"What? Oh aye, next time."

The sun's out. I get a bit thirsty as I'm walking home. There's a Coke machine. I get a can, lean on a lamp post. I keep looking round between sips and thinking about the Ointment. Don't want 'em creeping up on me.

I've been there about five minutes when I see two police officers walking towards me. I expect 'em to walk by, but they stop. One's a woman, other's a guy. The woman goes, "We been observing you, son. Why're you hanging around?"

I hold up the can. "Just having a drink and a breather."

The guy nods towards my pocket. "What you got in there?" I've kept one hand on Flicka all this time.

I grin. "Snake."

They both look hard at me. "You trying to be funny?" growls the guy.

I shake my head. "No, my snake's in here. See." Both officers take a step back as I pull Flicka out. "She's called Flicka," I tell them. "You can have a hold of her if you like."

Both police shake their heads. "You're right, son," says the woman. "What's your name?"

"Alex Cowan."

"Where d'you live?"

"Sellick House, Barn Hill."

"Number?"

"44."

"Right, well, you'd best be moving along. Oh." She nods at my can of Coke. "Be sure and dispose of that properly."

"How about that, Flicka?" I whisper as I put her back in my pocket and the police walk off. "Your first clash with the law." I know why they spoke to me, of course. I was hanging about looking nervous. And I'm wearing a hoody with something in the pocket. Maybe they thought I was dealing crack, like Burnie and his pals. Or maybe they thought I had a gun.

I wish.

Chapter 7
The Gang's All Here

Lying in bed that night, I'm like, *Out half the day today, no sign of Burn and his pals. Maybe he didn't really mean it when he told me I was dead. Maybe he just wanted to throw a scare into me.*

Don't ask me how I could even *think* that, after the way the guy'd terrorised me. Must've been half asleep or something.

Maybe I was dreaming. Anyway, I soon found out how serious he was.

Next morning, Tuesday, I'm tidying my room when my moby rings. "Hello?" I says, and a voice says, "Look out the window."

"Huh?" I says. "Who's this?" I know fine well who it is.

"The window," he says. "Look out."

I cross to the window, pull back the curtain. Zac Doyle's down there, leaning on the NO BALL GAMES sign. He lifts a hand, waves his cigarette at me. I drop the curtain. The voice on the phone says, "No more games, Cow. Today's the day. Like it says in the old song, *the gang's all here*." He laughs. "We've got the place surrounded, pal. A *cricket* couldn't get out of Sellick House without us knowing."

"Hey, listen, Mark," I burble. "It wasn't me who split on you in Next. I just happened to ..."

"Save your breath," he snarls, "you'll need it for crawling to Southern General." Southern General's our local hospital. Before I can say anything else, he cuts me off.

I chuck the moby on the bed, go on with my tidying. I'm on autopilot, too scared to notice what I'm doing. I'm supposed to go down Foodsave later for my mother, she's made a list. I can't go, but what will I tell her? That I don't feel well, or I've forgotten where Foodsave is? Will I say my legs've suddenly stopped working? Or do I tell the truth, which is that they *will* stop working when the Ointment gets hold of me?

I think, *Maybe if I stay in this morning, wait till afternoon to go out, they'll get fed up. It's got to be dead boring, just hanging around. The police might even see them, move them on.*

I'm kidding myself, of course. Mark Burn and his pals spend their *lives* hanging around. That's all they do and they know what they're doing. They know how to swap and change positions, so the police don't see the same guy in one spot for long.

In the end I settle for the *don't feel well* dodge with Ma. I used it a lot when I was still at school, to get a day off when the bullying was doing my head in. I'm an expert. The secret is to *act* unwell. *Saying* you feel bad sometimes works, but if you act in an odd way it works better. So, when I finish tidying my room I don't go into the kitchen and tell Ma I feel ill. I just lie down on the bed and wait. I know that sooner or later she'll start thinking what's wrong, why haven't I come out of my room? She'll call out for me, and I won't reply. That'll make her come to see me, me, and I'll be on my bed. I'll have my eyes closed, and I'll just mumble when she asks what's the matter. She'll fetch me something to drink, tell me to rest and go do her own shopping. I feel rotten about it, but what can I do?

It's twenty minutes before she calls out. "Alex?"

I don't answer.

"Alex, are you OK?" She thinks maybe I've sneaked out. I lie still.

"Alex?" She's starting to worry. Footfalls. She's coming up.

"Alex?" My eyes are closed but I know she's looking down at me. I groan, roll my head on the pillow. "I ... don't feel so good, Ma. Bit of a headache."

She lays a cool hand on my brow. "Hmmm. Where's the pain, son?"

"Back of the head, Ma. Near my neck."

"Aha. Throat sore at all?"

"Bit."

"Open your eyes, Alex."

I open my eyes and go, "Oooh."

"Light hurt, son?" She sounds worried, maybe I'm overdoing it.

"Aye, a wee bit. It's probably nothing. I'll just lie still for a while, OK?"

"I don't know, son. I think I'd best call Dr Brown, just to be on the safe side."

"No." I sit up. "It's nothing serious, Ma, really. If it was I'd know it."

She nods. "Well, you look fine and you've not got a temperature. We'll wait an hour and see how you go. Lie down and I'll make you some tea."

I feel really bad, having her make me tea and worry about me. But I'd feel a whole lot worse if I was half-way down Cameron Street and had Burnie chasing me.

After the tea I pretend I'm feeling a bit better. A peek outside shows me Mark Burn's by the NO BALL GAMES sign now. Zac's gone. I think about calling the police, telling 'em there's a guy dealing outside Sellick House, but I don't do it. They'd only think, *so what else is new*? And not come. I've just finished my tea when my phone goes.

"Hello?"

"I hope you're not thinking of letting your mammy do her *own* shopping, Cow?" says Burnie.

"What d'you mean?" I croak. "*What* shopping?"

"Don't give me that, Cow. It's Tuesday. Foodsave day, when you go trotting down the road with your list and your little plastic bag. We're all waiting. We're waiting for *you*, of course, but if you don't show up, your mammy'll do instead."

"What d'you mean, she'll do instead? Do for *what*?"

"Game of kneecap baseball, pal. You know what that is, don't you?"

"You wouldn't ... You can't ..."

Burn gives a nasty chuckle. "Oh, yes, I can, Cow," he goes on, "You *know* I can. How d'you think it'll make you feel, eh? Watching your mammy wobble around on crutches, knowing it should be your legs that got broken?"

"They'll know who did it," I shout. "The police, 'cos I'll tell 'em. You'll get ten years, you rotten ..."

He's gone. He's shut off his phone. Ma's in the lobby, putting her coat on. I get up and open my door. "Ma," I call out, "don't go out, I'll go. I'm OK now."

Tomorrow she'll have to nurse me for real. I won't have to pretend to be sick.

Chapter 8
Southeast

I force myself to act normal as I leave the flat and take the walkway to the stairs. Flicka's in my pocket. I don't know if that's a good idea but right now – dammit – I need a friend. My legs're shaking so badly I have to keep a hand on the wall in case I fall.

I haven't got a plan. No idea what I'll do once I'm out the door. I don't want to *go* out the door. Instinct screams at me not to. *Run!*

it yells inside my skull. *Hide while you can. If you stick your nose outside, you're dead.*

Think about Ma, says a little voice in my head. *In agony. Hospital. Crutches. All your fault.*

I've no choice, have I?

There's no one leaning on the NO BALL GAMES sign when I get downstairs. I stand on the bottom step, look all around. There's an old guy with a dog on a lead, and a big lass with two kids in a pushchair. No Ointment. No one else at all.

I start walking along the footpath that leads to Cameron Street. It's so still, it's creepy. I'm looking around every second, expecting Burn and his pals to jump out at me and come after me like a pack of hungry dogs. If they do, when they do, my only plan is to go like hell and hope I get to Foodsave before they run me down. They wouldn't attack me inside the place. They'd wait for me to come out. There's some stuff inside my head where the shop manager gets me a taxi to escape in, but it's just a dream. To be honest, I don't think I'll get as far as Foodsave anyway.

I get to Cameron Street, and nothing's happened yet. Something stirs inside me, feels like hope. Could it be that Mark Burn's just trying to scare me? That he doesn't mean to attack? Are the Ointment having a laugh right now and watching how I start and skitter at the smallest noise, like some hunted animal?

The hope is nice while it lasts, but it doesn't last long. Foodsave's at the corner of Cameron Street and Edmiston Drive. I'm crossing the car-park and just thinking how lucky I've been so far when I see Andy Crockett near the trolleys. He's clocked me, comes to meet me, grinning like the numpty he is. I go a different way, aiming for another entrance, and there's Jimmy Farr. He's standing by the door.

I turn and hurry back to the street. When I look round, Crockett's back by the trolleys and Jimmy hasn't budged.

I don't know what to do. There's a superstore on Paisley Road West. Maybe I can get Ma's stuff there. It's a bit of a trek, and I bet they'll try to ambush me on my way back but I'll give it a try. Nothing else I can do.

I'm not far down the road when I work out that a car's following me. Old white Polo. Maybe Burnie knows the owner or else they've boosted it. Probably they've boosted it. It's almost in the gutter, it's crawling so slowly to stay behind me. When I stop, it stops. Other drivers keep hooting at it, but it putters along and takes no notice. I don't look back, don't know who's in the car. I only know *I* don't want to be. I'm thinking about those gangster movies where a car pulls up beside the guy and some heavy says, "Get in. We're going for a ride." Then, next time you see the guy he's being fished out of the river. Our river's deep and wide and no more than ten minutes away. I really *don't* want to get in the car.

I think of a plan. It's dead simple. All I need is an alleyway. One of those back entries with a post in its mouth to stop drivers using it as a parking space or a rat-run. There's hundreds in every city. If I can find one in another minute or two, I'll be OK.

The Polo continues to crunch along at my heels, and it isn't long till we're just next to exactly the right sort of alleyway. I pretend I haven't seen it till my legs are almost touching the post. Then I hang a sudden left and break into a trot. I know the game's not over – they'll follow on foot, but I feel like laughing anyway. Mark Burn must've forgotten there are places cars can't go, the numpty.

As I exit the alley I look back. Two guys have followed me in, but they're not in a hurry. I turn right and slow to a walk. I don't know this part of town. I'm too far south of Cameron Street. I don't understand what Burn's playing at, but as soon as I get the chance I'd best start making my way back towards home.

That chance doesn't come. Mark Burn may be many things, but he's not daft. As I walk I become aware of a steady roar like a waterfall, except it isn't water, it's traffic. Non-stop, heavy traffic. The road the Ointment's steered me onto is a slip-road onto the flyovers and underpasses for all the fast traffic cutting across the city. There are no alleyways here, no pavements and no pedestrians. The only way back is the way

I've come, and the only way forward is to go underground through a lot of tunnels and underpasses. The tunnels are dark and they're empty.

They've set me a trap, and I've walked right into it.

Chapter 9
Underground Hardman Blues

I *so* don't want to go underground. I look behind, thinking, *Maybe I could …?* Maybe I could just get away? But no. Burnie knew I'd be looking to double back at this point. There are six people chasing me now – not all from the car. There are three on each side of the road. Four of them have baseball bats. As they walk along behind me they slap the bats onto their left palms, slap, slap, slap.

I can do two things – go underground, or go onto the flyover and try dodging the cars.

I walk down the ramp. When I come back up, it'll be on a stretcher. If at all. And if you think that's not the worst feeling in the world, you're crazy.

He's there, in front of me. I knew he would be, waiting for me once I've walked down the ramp. Andy Crockett's with him, but Burnie's got the bat. He doesn't want to share the joy of beating me up, not even with a pal. Kirsty Simpson's there as well, but I'm too scared to care about that.

"Hello, Cow," purrs Burnie. "I hope you made the most of that little walk, 'cos it's gonna be a wee while before you take another." He looks up and down at my legs with his pals all watching, grinning. Kirsty giggles. "Sorry you have to wait," he says. "I'm having trouble deciding which leg to do in first."

"C ... can you hang on a sec, Mark?" I've just remembered Flicka's in my hoody. What with one thing and another, I haven't even thought about her since I walked out the door at home. How I can think of her now I don't know. I just know I don't want her in my pocket when the Ointment start to beat me up.

"Hang on?" Burn gives a loud, harsh laugh. "What you gonna do, Cow? Say your prayers?"

"N ... no." I shake my head. "I just wanted to ... I don't want you to hurt Flicka. If I can just put her on the floor ..." I fish in my pocket, grab my pet, pull her out.

If I give you a million guesses, I bet you'll never guess what happens next. As I take Flicka out of my hoody, Burn's face goes drip white. The bat he's holding clatters to the floor as he reels back, with a scream. "Hang onto that thing, don't let go, don't let it near me!” I watch as he turns, staggers over to Kirsty, clings on to her and vomits down the back of her coat. I can’t believe what’s happening.

I don’t want to go on and on about it. Well yes, I *do*! I do want to go on about it, and I’m going to. Burn’s arms are round Kirsty’s neck and she’s trying to shove him off. She snorts and tries to push him away. Burn reeks of vomit and he’s making a real fool of himself. He smells disgusting. When Kirsty’s free, she peels off the ruined coat and chucks it at Burn. He bats it to one side and staggers towards her again with open arms. He’s blubbering something. It sounds like *I want my mammy*. And oh, you should see the look on Crockett’s face when the boss of the gang, his hero, needs his nappy changed. As for myself, I haven’t moved. I can’t move. I can’t believe how my luck’s changed. A minute ago I’d have given anything not to be down here. Now, I wouldn’t be anywhere else on Earth.

Old Burnie, you should've seen him. He's so spooked he doesn't know where he is. All he knows is, he wants to be somewhere else. He's phobic, see? About snakes. A lot of people are. Being phobic about snakes isn't all that odd. We all watch him, the three of us, and he totters up the ramp. He's still choking and he's bent over.

Chapter 10

A Penny Or Two Off The Crickets

It gets around, the story. Maybe it's the Ointment themselves blabbing, but myself I suspect Kirsty Simpson. You can be a fine-looking girl and still be a wee bit low on the loyalty front. And of course there's the matter of the ruined coat.

Anyway, the story gets around, and Burnie's street cred vanishes. If you're in a gang, you can't have a boss who cries for his mammy the minute someone waves a snake in his face. And if every softie you come across has a snake, then you're really in trouble. And that's what happens next.

It's Rab's idea. Remember Rab? He's the big guy, Mr Happy, charges for sand like it's gold-dust? And you know how some people can make money out of *any* situation? Well, Rab's one of those. Couple of weeks after Burnie's subway surprise, I'm in the shop for crickets and Rab says, "I heard about your pal."

I look at him. "Pal? What pal?"

"That Burn guy."

I shake my head. "No pal of mine."

Rab shrugs. “Whatever. You still seeking work?”

“Aye.”

“Well, I’ve got an idea to put to you.”

I pull a face. “Go on.”

“I’m thinking, the two of us, we could go into the personal security business.”

“Personal security?”

“Aye. See, that fella’s still out there. That Burn. You might think you’ve seen the last of him, but you’re wrong. Once a bully, always a bully. Before you know it, he’ll be back, and he’ll want to track down all the guys who’re laughing at him now. He won’t bother you – you’re the one with the snake.” Rab smiles and rubs his hands together. “But what if *all* the guys had snakes?”

“All the guys?”

"Aye. We could call 'em *pocket bodyguards*, something like that. You send the boys to me, I sell 'em their pocket bodyguards, we split the profit."

I shake my head. "It'd never work. Snakes're too expensive, and it's not just the snake. You need a tank, lamp, sand. Not to mention crickets at four quid a throw."

Rab shrugs. "I could give you a special price for snakes. I can do that if I'm shifting a lot – that's how supermarkets work. Sell loads – the price drops. I might even take a penny or two off the crickets. What d'you think?"

So now I'm in business with Rab, the miserable old so-and-so. We're not doing anything illegal. Dealing snakes isn't like crack or smack. And, what's more, we're keeping the streets peaceful. We don't see the Ointment any more. Jimmy's forgotten about smashing my elbows, and Burnie's keeping a very low profile. In fact Flicka's profile is higher than his, even when she's on the floor.

Barrington Stoke would like to thank all its readers for commenting on the manuscript before publication and in particular:

Callum Bailey
Sam Bridges
James Davis
Ben Dickinson
Kate Elliot
Skarz Hasakura
Christine Johnson
Philip Marsh
Nisa Patel
James Reid
Rajdeep Singh Ubee
Mabel Stewart
Darren Symon
Craig Watson
Alex White
Stephen Wong

Become a Consultant!

Would you like to give us feedback on our titles before they are published? Contact us at the email address below – we'd love to hear from you!

info@barringtonstoke.co.uk
www.barringtonstoke.co.uk

Snapshot

by Robert Swindells

Click. That's how easy it is. To take a photo. To change your life.

Victor didn't mean to get involved. You've got a camera in your hand, you see something happening, you take a photo, right? But someone wants these photos. *Bad.*

You vs Them. You know the streets. He knows there's a gun in his pocket. With a bullet just for you. Can Victor manage to stay alive?

Johnny Delgado: Private Detective

by Kevin Brooks

Two gorgeous girls in your bedroom, asking for help. What can you say? Except *yes*. Private Detective Johnny has his first case ... but it could be his last.

One rough tower block. Knives, drugs, a whole lot of dodgy deals. And no way out.

Welcome to Johnny's world. Enjoy the ride.

Johnny Delgado: Like Father, Like Son

by Kevin Brooks

A gang war is about to blow Johnny's estate apart. But Johnny's got problems of his own.

1) Find the man who killed his father

2) Find out why

3) Get revenge

The truth is out there. Johnny just needs to kick down a few doors to get to it ...

Until Proven Guilty

by Nigel Hinton

A dead girl. A murder charge.

Nathan's world has been blown apart.

Can he prove that the police are wrong?

Time is running out ....